BETRAYED IN SILK STOCKINGS

AN X-RATED NOVEL BY SAVANNAH WYLDE

CHAPTER ONE

The late-morning sun poured across the infinity pool like molten gold, turning every ripple into liquid fire. I stood barefoot on the warm travertine deck in my new white bikini—the one Victor had delivered yesterday in a cream silk box tied with black satin ribbon—and watched him cut through the water with slow, deliberate strokes.

He had brushed past me moments earlier on his way to the diving board. The back of his hand had grazed my bottom—not quite a swat, more a deliberate claim—and the brief contact sent a bright, electric flutter straight through my belly and down between my thighs. My sex gave a tiny, secret clench. I pressed my legs together and pretended to adjust the tie at my hip, but the tingling only grew.

Victor Kane. My temporary summer boss. Forty-nine years old, silver threading his dark hair, body still carved from years of boxing and whatever else powerful men do to stay dangerous. He reached the far end of the pool, braced his forearms on the edge, and looked back at me. Water streamed off the hard planes of his shoulders. Even from this distance those steel-gray eyes felt like fingers sliding under my bikini top.

I turned onto my stomach on the cushioned lounger and let my cheek rest on my folded arms. The sun baked my back; the faint chlorine scent mixed with coconut oil and the expensive bergamot cologne that always clung to him. Working for Victor was nothing like the boring office-temp jobs my friends had landed. This felt like stepping into someone else's fever dream.

He climbed the ladder. Water sheeted off him in glistening ropes. When he shook his head the droplets flew, some landing cool and sudden across my calves and the backs of my thighs. I squeaked.

"You're splashing me!"

"You're already wet, little Mia," he said, voice low and amused. He picked up one of the thick charcoal towels from the teak side table and dropped to one knee beside my lounger.

My heart kicked hard against my ribs. He was close enough now that I could smell the clean heat of his skin under the chlorine. The towel settled on my shoulder blades—soft, warm from the sun—and began to move in slow circles. Each pass dragged the terry cloth over skin still sensitive from the water, and every downward stroke tugged faintly at the thin ties of my bikini top.

I bit the inside of my lip. My nipples were already stiff little points pressing against the damp fabric. I told myself it was just the breeze off the canyon, but I knew better.

He worked lower, past the elastic waist of my bottoms, drying the length of my legs with the same unhurried care. When his palms cupped the undersides of my thighs I felt the breath leave my lungs in a soft rush. My sex pulsed once, hot and liquid, a slow seep of arousal soaking into the crotch of my suit. I squeezed my thighs together again, mortified and thrilled at the same time.

"You're dry now," I managed, voice higher than I wanted.

"Roll over." It wasn't a question.

My arms felt shaky as I pushed up and turned. The movement made my breasts sway inside the tiny triangles of white lycra. I lay back and looked up at him through my lashes. His eyes were on my mouth, then lower, tracing the rise of my chest with each quick breath I took.

He dropped the towel beside me and let his bare hand rest on my stomach—broad, warm, callused in places that spoke of real work once upon a time. He began to trace lazy spirals with his fingertips. Every circle pulled the skin of my belly tighter, sent little shivers racing up to my nipples and down to the needy place between my legs.

"You're shaking," he murmured.

"I'm… cold," I lied.

His mouth curved—just the smallest tilt. "Liar."

He slid his palm higher until the heel of his hand nudged the underside of my breast. My breath hitched. I could feel my pulse beating there, frantic and loud in my own ears. My sex clenched again, harder this time, and a fresh trickle of wetness slipped free. I was suddenly, shamefully aware of how swollen my lips felt, how the damp fabric clung and outlined every fold.

"Victor…" My voice came out small.

"Shh." He leaned closer. His beard brushed my collarbone as he spoke against my skin. "You've been watching me all morning, Mia. Every time I came up for air you were staring. Don't pretend you don't like my hands on you."

Heat flooded my cheeks, my chest, the tender insides of my thighs. I wanted to deny it. I wanted to be the good girl who would go back to college in the fall, who still blushed at dirty jokes in the dorm. But my body was telling a different story. My hips lifted—just a fraction—before I could stop them, pressing my mound toward his hand like a cat asking to be stroked.

He gave a low, satisfied sound in his throat. His fingers slipped under the edge of my bikini top and grazed the lower curve of my breast. My nipple scraped against his knuckle and I gasped—sharp, helpless. Pleasure arrowed straight to my clit. It felt huge, throbbing, trapped under the tight lycra.

"Someone might see," I whispered, glancing toward the glass walls of the house.

"No one's here but us." His thumb brushed back and forth across my nipple now, slow and deliberate. "And even if they were… I'd let them watch."

The words should have horrified me. Instead they made my inner walls flutter and squeeze around nothing. I could feel how slick I'd become, how the wetness had soaked through the fabric and was probably darkening it between my legs. I pressed my thighs together again, trapping his hand, and a tiny whimper escaped me.

He tugged the triangle of fabric aside. Cool air kissed my bare nipple an instant before his mouth closed over it. Hot. Wet. The flat of his tongue dragged across the aching peak and I arched off the lounger with a broken cry. My hands flew to his shoulders—not to push him away, but to hold on.

He sucked—gentle at first, then harder—and every pull felt like it was connected by invisible wires to the pulsing knot between my thighs. My hips rocked in tiny, helpless jerks. I was dripping now, slippery and swollen, every movement making the wet crotch of my bikini slide against my engorged clit.

When he finally lifted his head my nipple was dark red and glistening. He looked at my face—really looked—and whatever he saw made his pupils blow wide.

"Pretty little thing," he murmured. "So eager already."

His hand slid down my stomach, over the trembling plane of my abdomen, and cupped me through the soaked fabric. I jolted. The pressure against my clit was sudden and perfect. My thighs fell open without permission.

He rubbed—slow circles at first, then firmer strokes that dragged the slick lycra back and forth across my swollen bud. Every pass sent sparks shooting up my spine. My breathing turned ragged; small, needy sounds slipped out of me with every exhale.

"Victor… please…"

"Please what, baby?" His voice was gravel. "Please stop? Or please don't?"

I couldn't answer. My hips were chasing his hand now, grinding shamelessly against his palm. The wet fabric made obscene little sucking noises with every movement.

I felt swollen everywhere—lips, clit, the tight mouth of my entrance that had never known anything but my own fingers.

He hooked two fingers under the crotch of my bikini and pulled it aside. Cool air hit my bare sex and I whimpered at the sudden exposure. Then his fingertips were there—sliding through my drenched folds, parting me, finding the slippery entrance and pressing just inside.

My whole body seized. One long, trembling moan tore out of my throat. He was barely in—just the tips of two fingers—but the stretch, the heat, the knowing pressure against my untouched walls made stars burst behind my eyelids.

"So tight," he growled against my throat. "So fucking wet for me already."

He crooked his fingers, stroking that sensitive place inside while his thumb found my clit again. The dual sensation was too much. My thighs shook. My toes curled against the lounger. Pressure built fast—too fast— coiling low in my belly like a spring wound to breaking.

"I—I'm going to—" The words dissolved into a sob.

"Come for me, Mia." His mouth was at my ear now, voice dark velvet. "Let me feel this sweet little cunt come all over my fingers."

He pressed deeper, rubbed harder, and the spring snapped.

I came with a sharp, keening cry—back arching, hips bucking, inner walls clamping and fluttering wildly around his invading fingers. Wetness surged, coating his hand, trickling down the crease of my ass. Wave after wave rolled through me until I was shaking, gasping, tears of pure overwhelmed pleasure slipping from the corners of my eyes.

When the last tremor finally faded I collapsed back against the cushions, chest heaving, skin flushed and slick with sweat and pool water and my own release.

Victor withdrew his fingers slowly. I whimpered at the loss. He brought them to his mouth and licked them clean—slow, deliberate—while he watched my face.

"Delicious," he said simply.

Then he leaned down and kissed me—soft at first, then deeper, letting me taste myself on his tongue.

I kissed him back like I was drowning.

I didn't know then that this was only the beginning.

That the man who had just made me come harder than I ever had in my life was already planning exactly how he would ruin me.

And that I would beg him to do it.

CHAPTER TWO

"That was nice," I whispered, my voice soft and dreamy, floating somewhere above my still-trembling body. Every inch of me felt warm and liquid, like I'd been dipped in sunlight and honey. "Are you… finished…?"

Victor gave that low, dangerous chuckle that always made my stomach flutter. He rose onto his knees, straddling my ribs so the heavy heat of him rested right between my bare breasts. Even half-soft, his cock felt enormous against my skin—thick, warm, still slick from my mouth and his release.

"No way, kitten," he murmured, eyes dark with fresh hunger. "I was just getting started. I've got a lot more for you."

He rubbed the smooth, sticky head slowly back and forth across one nipple, then the other. The friction sent sharp little aftershocks racing down to my clit. I whimpered—high and helpless—and felt a fresh trickle of wetness slip from between my swollen folds.

"Are you ready for more?" His voice had gone husky, commanding.

I couldn't speak. My throat was still raw from trying to take all of him. I could only nod, eyes wide, lips parted and tingling.

He reached behind my neck and tugged the last knot of my bikini top. The tiny triangles fell away. My breasts spilled free into the bright afternoon light, nipples already tight and aching from his earlier attention. Victor groaned deep in his chest—a sound that vibrated straight through me—and pressed himself between the soft mounds, squeezing them together until I cradled his thickening length in warm flesh.

The slide of him was obscene and perfect. Every slow drag tugged at my sensitive skin, made my nipples throb harder. I squirmed beneath him, thighs rubbing together, desperate for any pressure at all on my pulsing clit.

"You're a hot little thing, aren't you?" he said, watching my face with heavy satisfaction.

My cheeks burned, but the words lit something wicked inside me. I pressed my breasts tighter around him, loving how his breath caught.

"Say it," he ordered, voice dropping to that low growl I already craved. "Tell me what you are, Mia."

I swallowed hard. My hips rolled uselessly against the towel. "I'm… I'm hot," I breathed.

"More." No smile now—just steel wrapped in velvet. "Say it right."

The filthy phrase felt huge in my mouth, but saying it made my whole body clench with shameful excitement. "I'm a horny little bitch," I whispered, barely audible. "And I'm hot for your cock."

His grin was slow and triumphant. "Good girl."

He eased off me then, lying back on the thick lounge cushion so the sun painted every hard line of his body in gold. His cock—already swelling again—stood proud and dark against his stomach, glistening at the tip. My mouth watered instantly.

"First you take care of me," he said, "then I'll take care of you."

My hands shook as I crawled between his spread thighs. "How…?"

"Suck my dick, kitten." The blunt words hit me like a slap of heat. "Then I'll eat that sweet virgin pussy until you scream for me."

My head spun. I'd never even thought about doing something so dirty, yet the idea of tasting him again—of making him groan because of my mouth—set my whole body trembling.

"I've… never done that before," I admitted in a tiny voice, eyes locked on the thick vein that pulsed along his shaft.

"You'll do fine." He caught my wrist and guided my hand to the base of him. "Start with kisses. Nice and wet. Show me how much you want to please me."

I leaned down, heart hammering so loud I was sure he could hear it. My lips brushed the smooth, hot crown. He tasted of salt and something darker, richer—himself. A thick bead of precum welled at the slit; I flicked my tongue out to catch it and moaned softly at the intimate, musky flavor.

Victor sucked in a sharp breath. "That's it. All over me, baby."

Emboldened, I kissed down the length of him—soft, open-mouthed, leaving shiny trails. When I reached the heavy sac beneath I hesitated, then cradled his balls gently in one palm. They felt warm, full, alive under my fingers. I kissed them too, then dragged the flat of my tongue all the way back up in one long, slow stroke.

His hips jerked. "Fuck, Mia…"

The rough praise melted something inside me. I wrapped my fingers around the thick base—God, my hand couldn't even close—and swirled my tongue around the swollen head again, bolder now, sucking just the tip between my lips like hard candy. More precum coated my tongue; I swallowed greedily, humming around him.

He groaned louder, fingers sliding into my hair—not pulling, just guiding. "Deeper. Show me you can take it."

I hollowed my cheeks and slid down farther. The fat head nudged the back of my throat too soon; I gagged, eyes watering, and pulled back with a wet, gasping pop.

His grip tightened just enough to make my scalp tingle. "Breathe through your nose. Relax your throat. You can do it."

Tears clung to my lashes, but the ache between my legs had turned unbearable. I wanted to be good. I wanted him to lose control because of me.

I tried again—slower—relaxing as best I could. Inch by inch he filled my mouth until my lips stretched wide and my nose brushed coarse dark hair. My throat worked convulsively; saliva drooled from the corners of my mouth and ran down his shaft in shiny rivulets.

"Jesus Christ," he rasped, hips lifting in tiny helpless thrusts. "Look at you… my perfect little cocksucker."

The filthy word sent lightning straight to my clit. Without thinking I slipped my free hand between my own thighs, rubbing frantically over the soaked crotch of my bikini bottoms while I bobbed—awkward at first, then hungrier, sloppier.

Victor watched me touch myself and his control visibly frayed. "That's it. Play with that greedy little cunt while you choke on my cock."

I moaned around his thickness, the vibration making him curse. My fingers slipped under the fabric; I found my clit swollen and slippery and circled it desperately. The pressure built fast—too fast.

He felt me shaking. "You're gonna come just from sucking me off, aren't you?"

I whimpered yes around him, head moving faster, tears streaming now but I didn't care.

"Then come," he growled. "Come with my dick down your throat, kitten."

The command shattered me. My whole body seized; I cried out muffled against his flesh as sharp, blinding pleasure ripped through me. My pussy clenched and fluttered, soaking my fingers, dripping onto the towel.

Victor's restraint snapped. He gripped my head with both hands now, fucking shallowly into my mouth while I shuddered through the aftershocks. "Fuck—here it comes—take every drop—"

Hot, thick spurts flooded my tongue again. I swallowed instinctively, gulping down pulse after pulse until my head spun and my eyes watered from lack of air. When he finally eased back, a final rope painted my lips and chin. I licked it up automatically, dazed and blissful.

He collapsed onto his back, chest heaving. I crawled up beside him, laying my cheek on his shoulder, still tasting him everywhere—on my tongue, my lips, the back of my throat.

For a long minute we simply breathed together under the warm sun.

Then he turned his head, brushed sweat-damp hair from my flushed face, and smiled that slow, dangerous smile.

"That was beautiful, Mia," he murmured, tracing a fingertip along my swollen lower lip. "But we're not done. Not even close."

My heart stuttered—half fear, half illicit thrill—at the dark promise in his voice.

I should have asked what he meant.

Instead I pressed closer, and asked: "Are you going to do me now?".

"Sure thing, baby," he said, lifting himself up onto his elbow so he could see all of me. "Didn't I promise you?"

Just then, the phone rang.

CHAPTER THREE

"But you promised!" I wailed, my voice breaking like thin glass, the hurt sharp in my chest.

"Shut your mouth and do what you're told," Victor snarled, his fingers clamping around my upper arm like steel bands. He hauled me upright so fast the world tilted; my bare feet scrabbled on the hot flagstones. "It's my private line—could be important." Another rough shove sent me stumbling toward the open French doors, his big palm cracking across my ass with a sound like a whip. The sting bloomed instantly, hot and bright, racing straight to my already throbbing clit even as tears pricked my eyes.

He turned and sliced into the pool with a clean dive, water exploding around his muscled shoulders, washing away the sheen of sweat and the salty traces of my mouth that still lingered on his skin. I'd licked him clean only minutes ago, every thick, musky drop, my tongue trembling with eagerness and something darker I couldn't name.

I dragged the silk robe—his robe—over my shoulders. It was far too large, the heavy charcoal fabric whispering against my sensitive nipples, the hem grazing the tops of my thighs. Barefoot, legs shaky, pussy still swollen and slick from his earlier teasing, I padded across the cool marble into the dim, air-conditioned hush of the mansion. My heart hammered. One moment he'd been almost gentle, murmuring praise against my throat; the next he'd shoved me away like I was nothing. It stung deeper than the slap.

He's under pressure, I told myself, making excuses the way girls do. He runs empires—import-export deals, high-end hospitality services for very important clients. I'm just the summer secretary, the girl he picked up because I type ninety words a minute and look good in a short skirt. I don't know the details. I don't need to.

"Victor Kane Enterprises," I answered, trying to sound crisp and efficient even with the taste of his come still coating my tongue, thick and faintly bitter.

"Who the fuck is this?" The voice on the other end was gravel and impatience.

"Mr. Kane's secretary. He's… occupied right now. May I ask who's calling?"

"Tell your fancy-ass boss it's Dante. And tell him to get his fucking ass on the phone right now. It's urgent."

I flinched at the casual profanity. No one had ever spoken to me like that—not in high school, not even the roughest boys at senior parties. My cheeks burned.

Before I could respond, Victor strode in, still toweling water from his broad shoulders, droplets glittering on the dark hair of his chest. I pressed the hold button.

"It's someone named Dante," I said softly. "He was… very rude."

Victor muttered something sharp under his breath and snatched the phone.

I released the hold.

"Yeah, Dante—what? …What? …Jesus Christ." His voice dropped to something dangerous. He listened, jaw working, then slammed the receiver down.

He began pacing—long, predatory strides across the Persian rug—alternately raking fingers through his damp hair and slamming one fist into the opposite palm.

"Fucking Feds... cocksuckers..."

"Victor?" My voice came out small, frightened. "Is everything okay?"

He whirled, eyes blazing with such raw fury that I actually stepped back, robe slipping off one shoulder. For a heartbeat I thought he might hit me.

Then the mask snapped back into place—cool, controlled, almost tender. He closed the distance, slid a heavy arm around my shoulders, thumb stroking the nape of my neck in slow circles that raised gooseflesh down my spine.

"Nothing for you to worry about, sweetheart. Bad news on a deal, that's all. I forgot myself for a second." His voice dropped, intimate. "Why don't we finish what we started? I've got meetings stacked all afternoon... and I did make you a promise."

* * *

My whole body trembled as he guided me up the sweeping staircase to one of the guest suites—the pale-gray one with the long balcony overlooking the gated driveway and the palm-lined approach. The room smelled of clean linen and faint citrus from the diffuser on the dresser. Sunlight poured through sheer curtains, turning the massive bed into a golden island.

He slipped the robe from my shoulders. It whispered to the carpet. Then he eased me down onto the cool sheets, gentle now, almost careful. The contrast after his earlier roughness made my head swim. I almost forgot the flash of violence downstairs.

"Are you sure... right now?" I whispered, nerves fluttering like trapped birds in my belly.

"Of course, baby." His hand slid between my thighs without preamble. My labia were still puffy, slick with arousal. His fingertips parted me, dipping into the wet heat, tracing delicate circles around my entrance before brushing upward to press lightly against my hymen. The touch sent a bright, electric jolt through me—part ache, part hunger.

"And you want it too," he murmured, watching my face. "I can feel how wet you are for me."

"Yes," I moaned, hips lifting helplessly into his hand. "God, yes... I do."

He spread me wider with one hand; with the other he explored deeper, stroking the slick inner walls, teasing the fragile barrier until I whimpered. Every glide of his fingers made my clit throb, made fresh cream seep from me.

"Do it," I begged, shameless. "Please do it, Victor."

"Do what, Mia?" His voice was velvet over steel, eyes locked on mine. "Tell me exactly. Use the words."

Heat flooded my face, but the need was stronger. "Eat me," I whispered, then louder, trembling: "Eat my pussy... please."

The filthy phrase hung between us, making my nipples tighten to aching points and my inner walls flutter. His pupils blew wide; I saw his cock twitch against his thigh, already thickening again.

He bent to one breast first, tongue circling the pale-pink areola in slow, wet spirals until the nipple stood rigid. Then the other, laving the soft mound until both glistened, heavy and sensitive. Each lick sent pulses straight to my core; my breasts felt swollen, almost too full.

"You like that, baby girl?"

"Oooooh, yes..." I arched, offering more. "Suck them... suck my tits... and my cunt..."

He growled low in his throat and covered me, mouth ravenous. Gentle suction at first, then harder pulls that made my back bow. I creamed instantly, hot juice trickling down my ass crack, soaking the sheets. My whole body shook with the promise of something bigger than anything I'd felt before.

"Bite them," I gasped. "Bite my fucking tits!"

His teeth closed—sharp, deliberate—sending a white-hot line of pleasure-pain straight to my clit. I thrashed, dragging his mouth to the other nipple, craving the sting again. He bit harder, tasting the faint metallic tang of blood. His fingers plunged deeper, stretching my cherry, pinching my swollen clit until stars burst behind my eyelids.

"Oh God—Victor!"

He marked me—red bites blooming across my breasts, down my ribs, over the quivering plane of my stomach. Every nip made my hips jerk, mouth slack, drool slipping from the corners.

"My pussy," I whimpered. "Please... eat my poor little pussy..."

His hands stroked my thighs, thumbs digging into the soft inner flesh. He nibbled the crease where leg met hip; the rich, sweet scent of my arousal filled the air. I felt his hot breath ghost over my slit and shuddered violently.

He parted my folds with rough thumbs and sealed his mouth over me. I bucked hard, crying out as his tongue slithered through the wetness, lapping my clit, then plunging inside to circle my cherry.

"Oooooooooooh... yessssss!"

Cream drenched his face. He groaned into my flesh, the vibration making my clit pulse wildly. Hands gripping my ass, he lifted me, holding me open while his tongue fucked in and out, swirling, sucking, teasing.

"Bite me... lick me... suck me off!" The words spilled out, obscene and desperate.

He obeyed—teeth grazing my swollen lips, nipping the clit, then drawing the throbbing bud between his lips, tugging rhythmically. I screamed, thighs clamping his head like a vise.

He tormented me—nipping, licking, holding me

teetering on the brink until tears streamed down my temples. "Please... I can't... make me come!"

Fingers found my ass, tickling the tight ring while his teeth sank into my clit and his tongue whipped mercilessly.

The orgasm detonated—searing white lightning that tore through every nerve, my virgin cunt spasming, gushing thick cream over his tongue, down his chin. I thrashed wildly, pounding the mattress, back arched so hard I thought I'd snap.

"I'm coming! I'm coming! Oh God, Victor—I'm commmiiinnnggg!"

He held me down, sucking harder, stretching my clit with his lips while fingers probed my ass. Another climax crashed on the heels of the first—fiercer, blinding. My body convulsed like I was breaking apart.

He ravaged me through it, chewing my cunt flesh, poking my untouched hole, groaning as my spasms milked his tongue. My thighs locked around his ears; I couldn't let go, couldn't stop the endless, rolling ecstasy.

When the waves finally ebbed I lay limp, twitching, chest heaving, pussy still fluttering in sweet aftershocks.

"Oh... Victor..." It was all I could manage.

He sat back, wiping his drenched face, cock thick and dark with blood, throbbing in his fist. He shook it at me, eyes gleaming with dark promise.

"Wait till you feel this splitting you open."

"But... I'm still a virgin..."

"Not for long, baby." His smile was slow, possessive, predatory. "Not for long."

My heart slammed against my ribs—fear and longing twisting together until I couldn't tell them apart. He'd unlocked something inside me, something hungry and bottomless. But the certainty in his voice, the way he looked at me like I already belonged to him...it frightened me more than I wanted to admit.

"Don't you have those meetings soon?" I asked, voice small, grasping for any delay.

"Yeah," he conceded, glancing toward the balcony doors where the palms swayed against the bright sky. "But they won't take all day."

CHAPTER FOUR

The shower jets stung my skin with icy needles, washing away the sticky evidence of what Victor had done to me that morning. Through the frosted glass I could see his tall silhouette moving—adjusting his cuffs, sliding into the charcoal suit jacket that made him look even more untouchable.

"Come down when you're finished, Mia," he called without turning. "I may need you to take dictation."

The bedroom door clicked softly behind him.

I turned the temperature up until steam clouded the mirror and let the heat cascade over my breasts, my stomach, the tender insides of my thighs. The water felt almost tender after Victor's rough hands, after the way he'd stretched and filled me until I'd sobbed with something between pain and gratitude. My body still hummed, raw and oversensitive, every droplet that struck my nipples sending tiny aftershocks straight to my clit.

I stepped out, skin prickling, and wrapped myself in the thick white robe he'd left folded on the vanity. My bikini and sundress were still downstairs in the pool cabana; I'd have to slip down later. For now the robe would do.

Through the bedroom window I watched a sleek black Mercedes glide up the circular drive. A man and a woman stepped out. He wore a fitted leather jacket over dark denim, casual but expensive. She… she looked like sin poured into fabric. Tiny white shorts, a black halter that barely contained her breasts, crimson stilettos clicking on the stone path. Even from the second floor I could see the glossy black stockings shimmering on her long legs.

My breath caught. I didn't know why the sight of her stockings made my belly flutter the way it did.

I was still toweling my hair when the bedroom door opened without a knock.

She stepped inside alone.

Up close she was even more overwhelming. Jet hair falling in heavy waves, lips the color of fresh blood, hazel eyes that seemed to see straight through the robe to the damp skin beneath. The spicy-vanilla scent of her perfume wrapped around me like warm smoke.

"Hello, little dove," she said. Her voice was low, smoky, almost a caress. "Victor asked me to come keep you company. Apparently he doesn't need you downstairs after all."

I clutched the robe tighter. "Oh. Okay."

She closed the door with a soft click and crossed the room on those impossible heels. Every step made the sheer black silk of her stockings whisper against itself. The sound went straight between my legs.

"I'm Raven," she said, sitting on the edge of the bed and crossing one long leg over the other. The motion drew my eyes to the dark band of her garter peeking beneath the hem of her shorts. "And you're Mia."

I nodded, cheeks burning.

She tilted her head, studying me. "You still smell like sex and chlorine. Delicious combination."

I didn't know what to say to that. My tongue felt thick.

Raven reached into the sleek leather tote she'd carried in and drew out a flat black gift box tied with scarlet ribbon.

"Victor mentioned you've been… improvising with your wardrobe." A small, knowing smile. "We can do better than sundresses and flip-flops if you're going to be working closely with him."

She untied the ribbon with one scarlet nail and lifted the lid.

Inside lay folded black silk—stockings so sheer they looked like liquid shadow, a matching garter belt of delicate black lace, and a bra-and-panty set that was more suggestion than coverage. The panties were barely there: a tiny triangle of silk in front, thin straps that would disappear between my cheeks. The bra was balconette style, designed to lift and frame rather than conceal.

My mouth went dry.

"Private secretaries in this house don't wear cotton," Raven said softly. "They wear silk. It feels different. It moves differently. It reminds you, every second you're wearing it, exactly who you belong to."

She stood and held out the stockings. "Let me show you."

I should have said no. I should have asked questions. Instead my hands moved almost by themselves, untying the robe belt. The terrycloth fell open. Cool air kissed my still-damp nipples and they drew into tight little peaks instantly.

Raven's gaze slid down my body like a physical touch.

"Beautiful," she murmured. "Now sit."

I perched on the edge of the vanity stool. She knelt—graceful even in those heels—and lifted my right foot. The stocking was impossibly light, cool against my skin as she gathered it into a soft ring and slipped it over my toes.

The silk glided up my calf like a lover's tongue.

I gasped.

Every tiny nerve in my leg woke up at once. The fabric was so fine it felt like cool water pouring over me, yet it hugged every curve, every muscle, caressing me in a way no cotton ever had. When she smoothed it behind my knee and drew it higher, up the sensitive inside of my thigh, I had to bite my lip to keep from whimpering.

The silk kissed the crease where thigh met groin and I felt my pussy clench, already slick again.

Raven fastened the garter straps—one front, one back—with deft fingers. Each tiny snap sent a jolt through me. Then she repeated the ritual on my left leg. By the time both stockings were in place I was trembling, thighs pressed together, trying to hide how wet I'd become.

She rose and stepped behind me. In the mirror I watched her hands slide the bra straps up my arms. The cups lifted my breasts, framing them like an offering. The silk was so thin my nipples showed through, dark pink shadows against black.

The panties came last.

She knelt again, this time between my parted knees.

"Lift," she whispered.

I raised my hips. Raven drew the tiny scrap of silk up my legs. The front panel settled against my mound, barely covering anything; the back disappeared between my cheeks, a thin ribbon of silk nestling against my asshole. The sensation was obscene—cool, slippery, invasive. Every tiny shift of my hips rubbed the silk against my clit and I had to grip the edge of the vanity to keep from moaning aloud.

Raven stood behind me again. In the mirror our eyes met.

"How does it feel?" she asked, voice husky.

I swallowed. "Like… like I'm naked and dressed at the same time. Like every inch of me is being touched."

Her smile was slow, predatory.

"That's the point, little dove."

She stepped closer. Her breasts brushed my back through her halter. One hand slid down my stomach, over the garter belt, and cupped me through the silk panties. The heat of her palm pressed the fabric against my swollen clit.

I whimpered.

"You're soaking through already," she murmured against my ear. "Such a responsive little thing."

Her fingers moved in slow circles. The silk slid over

my clit like liquid fire. I could feel every ridge of her fingerprints through the thin material. My hips rocked forward without permission, chasing the pressure.

Raven laughed softly. "Victor's going to love seeing you like this. But first…"

She turned me to face her.

Her mouth closed over mine—slow, deep, tasting of lipstick and sin. Her tongue stroked mine while her hands roamed my silk-covered body, tracing the straps, the garters, the places where stocking met bare thigh. Every touch felt amplified, electric. The silk transmitted heat and pressure in ways bare skin never could.

When she finally pulled back I was panting, pupils blown, thighs trembling.

"On the bed," she said. "On your back. Legs apart."

I obeyed without thought.

The silk stockings slid against the sheets with a faint hiss that made my clit throb. Raven crawled over me, straddling one thigh, her own stockings rasping against mine. The friction was unbearable.

She leaned down and kissed the slope of one breast above the bra cup, then bit—gently at first, then harder. I arched, crying out. The silk bra offered no protection; her teeth felt sharper, more intimate.

"You taste like summer," she whispered, moving lower. "And you're going to taste even better when I'm finished."

Her mouth closed over my clit through the panties.

The silk turned the sensation into something torturously diffuse and yet piercingly focused. I could feel the heat of her tongue, the wet drag of it, but filtered through that maddeningly thin barrier. I bucked against her face, hands fisting the sheets.

Raven hooked the crotch of the panties aside with one finger.

Then her mouth was on me—bare, hot, relentless.

I screamed.

She licked and sucked and nibbled until my whole world narrowed to the wet heat of her tongue and the silk still clinging to my legs like a second skin. Every time I shifted, the stockings stroked me, reminding me how completely I'd been dressed for pleasure, for display, for surrender.

When I came it felt like the orgasm started in my toes, raced up the silk-sheathed columns of my legs, and detonated in my core. I thrashed, sobbing her name, drenching her chin while the stockings whispered against the sheets with every convulsion.

Raven lifted her head at last, lips glossy, eyes glittering.

"Silk suits you, Mia," she purred. "You were made for it."

I lay there panting, legs still trembling inside their black sheaths, heart hammering against ribs that felt too small to contain everything I was feeling.

And somewhere deep inside, a small, treacherous voice whispered that I never wanted to take them off.

Not ever.

CHAPTER FIVE

The bedroom door opened without a knock.

"Having fun, girls?"

Victor Kane's voice rolled through the room like distant thunder—low, amused, and edged with possession. I jerked upright on the bed, silk sheets sliding off my flushed skin. My heart slammed against my ribs. Instinctively I tried to pull the thin satin coverlet over my breasts, as though a scrap of fabric could hide what Raven and I had just done.

Raven only laughed—that slow, smoky sound that always made my stomach flutter. She stretched languidly beside me, not bothering to cover herself. Her heavy breasts shifted with the movement, dark nipples still glistening from my mouth.

"Don't be shy now, kitten," she purred, trailing one scarlet nail down my bare thigh. "Victor doesn't mind sharing his toys. He *likes* watching them play."

I looked toward the doorway, cheeks burning. Victor stood there in his charcoal suit, collar open, silver threading his dark hair at the temples. Behind him loomed the man who's arrived with Raven—leather jacket stretched across wide shoulders, dark denim hugging his thighs, that same quiet intensity in his brown eyes that had unsettled me the first time we met.

"Hi, Mia," he said softly over Victor's shoulder. His

gaze slid over me—slow, deliberate, almost tender—and something inside me clenched.

Victor's eyes narrowed. "Dante. Take Raven and get out. I have business."

Raven sighed theatrically and swung her long, stocking-clad legs off the bed. She stood in one fluid motion, garter straps snapping faintly against her olive thighs. She bent to retrieve her black pencil skirt and emerald silk blouse from the floor, dressing with the reverse grace of a stripper who knows every eye is on her.

"Fine, boss," she drawled, giving Victor a knowing wink as she buttoned the blouse over her still-hard nipples. "Just don't break the little one before the rest of us get another turn."

"Out," Victor said flatly. The word carried no room for argument.

Dante stepped forward, fingers closing gently but firmly around Raven's elbow. As they passed me, his eyes met mine again. This time he gave the smallest, almost imperceptible wink—not leering, not crude. It felt… conspiratorial. Like a secret offered in silence. My breath caught. Heat bloomed low in my belly despite the fear prickling my skin.

The door clicked shut.

Victor turned to me. His steel-gray eyes were cold now, the amusement gone.

"Out by the pool I thought you liked cock, Mia." His voice was quiet, dangerous. "Thought I'd found myself a sweet little virgin. Not some eager little dyke."

The word hit like a slap. Tears stung my eyes instantly.

"No—Victor, please—" My voice cracked. "I thought… Raven said you wanted me to… to learn. To please you."

He crossed the room in two strides. His open palm cracked across my cheek—sharp, stinging. I crumpled to my knees on the carpet, one hand flying to my burning face, the other clutching the sheet to my chest.

"I don't keep dykes on payroll," he snarled. "Maybe Raven can find you work licking cunt for pocket change."

"No!" The word tore out of me, desperate. Tears spilled hot down my cheeks. "Please—I thought that's what you wanted. I did it for you. I'll do anything. Take my cherry, Victor. Take it now. Please. Fuck me. Make me yours."

I crawled forward on my knees, silk stockings whispering against the carpet, and wrapped my arms around his legs. I pressed my wet cheek to the fine wool of his trousers, trembling.

He looked down at me for a long moment. Then he laughed—low, satisfied.

"So easy," he murmured. "Even easier than I thought."

His fingers twisted into my long blonde hair, yanking my head back so I had to meet his eyes. The pull burned my scalp, but the pain only made the ache between my legs sharper.

"You really want it, don't you, kitten?"

"Yes," I breathed. "Yes, Victor. Let me prove how much I need you."

He pulled me to my feet by my hair. His mouth crashed down on mine—brutal, claiming. I melted against him, opening for his tongue, tasting whiskey and danger. His free hand tore the sheet away, leaving me naked except for the sheer black garter belt, silk stockings, and the lacy thong Raven had made me keep on.

My fingers shook as I fumbled with his belt. The buckle clinked. I dragged his zipper down, shoved his trousers and briefs to his ankles in one frantic motion. His cock sprang free—heavy, thick, already rigid. A ragged moan escaped me.

"It's so big," I whispered, licking my lips. "So hard…"

He kicked off his shoes, stepped free of his clothes, and dropped onto the wide bed, leaning back against the headboard like a king.

"Suck it first," he ordered. "Get it nice and wet for that virgin cunt."

I climbed onto the bed, knees sinking into the mattress. The silk of my stockings slid against the sheets as I crawled between his spread thighs. I wrapped both hands around his shaft—hot, velvet steel—and lowered my mouth.

The first taste of him—salty, musky, male—flooded my senses. I moaned around the head, swirling my tongue, sucking greedily. My pussy clenched emptily, soaking the thin strip of lace between my thighs.

Victor groaned. One big hand slid down my back, over the curve of my ass, fingers tracing the garter straps before dipping between my legs. He tugged the thong aside and pressed two thick fingers into my dripping folds.

"Enough," he rasped. "I want that pussy now."

I whimpered, reluctant to let him go, but I obeyed. I swung one leg over his hips, straddling him. My stockings shimmered in the low light as I positioned myself above his cock. The swollen head kissed my slick entrance through the torn lace.

"Careful, kitten," he growled, teeth gritted. "Don't strangle me before I get inside."

I rocked forward. The fat head parted my folds, pressing against the fragile barrier inside me. My whole body quaked.

"I'm going to be yours," I breathed, trembling.

Victor's hands clamped onto my hips. "You already are."

He yanked me down.

Pain tore through me—white-hot, searing. My cherry gave way in one brutal instant. I screamed, nails digging into his shoulders, body arching like a bowstring. Tears streamed down my face.

"Victor—Victor—it hurts—"

"Shh." His voice softened—just a fraction. One hand cupped my breast, thumb circling my aching nipple. "Breathe. Move slow. Get used to me."

I sobbed, shaking, but I obeyed. Tiny rocks of my hips at first—each motion stretching the raw, burning place where we were joined. Slowly, impossibly, the pain began to blur into something else. Heat. Fullness. A deep, pulsing ache that made me whimper for more.

"I can feel you," I gasped. "So deep… throbbing inside me…"

"That's it." His hands tightened on my hips. "Ride it, kitten. Show me how much you want to be my whore."

The word should have shamed me. Instead it lit me up. I lifted and slammed back down, crying out as his cock filled me again and again. My breasts bounced, nipples tight and stinging. The garter belt dug into my hips with every thrust. Silk stockings slid against his thighs.

"Harder," I begged. "Please—harder—"

Victor growled low in his throat. In one motion he rolled us, pinning me beneath him. His weight crushed me into the mattress, cock never leaving my body. He hooked my stockinged legs over his elbows, spreading me wide.

"You want it rough?" he rasped, pulling almost all the way out before slamming back in.

"Yes—God, yes!"

He fucked me like he owned me—long, punishing strokes that drove the breath from my lungs. My pussy fluttered and clenched, slick and greedy. Every thrust punched against something deep inside that made stars burst behind my eyes.

"I'm—oh God—I'm going to come—" I wailed.

"Come on my cock," he snarled. "Milk me, kitten. Show me what a good little slut you are."

The orgasm hit like a freight train. My back bowed, heels drumming against his back, stockings rasping.

My cunt convulsed around him, gushing slick heat. I screamed his name until my voice broke.

Victor's rhythm faltered. His cock swelled impossibly thicker. With a guttural groan he buried himself to the root and erupted—hot, thick spurts flooding my ravaged pussy. Each pulse dragged another aftershock from me until I was limp, trembling, filled.

He stayed inside me a long moment, breathing hard, silver-streaked hair damp against his forehead.

Then he pulled out slowly. I whimpered at the loss, feeling his come trickle out of me, soaking the sheets beneath my hips.

Victor looked down at me—flushed, wrecked, silk stockings laddered now, garters twisted—and gave a slow, satisfied smile.

"Good girl," he murmured, brushing sweat-damp hair from my face. "Very good girl."

I stared up at him, heart pounding, body still shivering with aftershocks.

And somewhere deep inside, a small, treacherous voice whispered that I would do anything—*anything*—to feel that owned again.

CHAPTER SIX

The days melted together like warm wax, and I found myself sinking deeper into Victor Kane's world with every sunrise. I was at the sprawling glass-and-marble estate on the cliffs almost around the clock—taking dictation in his soundproof study, typing encrypted memoranda on the computer he'd given me, then slipping out of my suit and lingerie to float naked in the infinity pool that overlooked the Pacific, the salt air kissing my skin while I waited for him to finish whatever "business" kept him behind closed doors.

Evenings were different. Victor would appear in one of his immaculate charcoal suits, pull me against him, and murmur that we were going out. He draped me in things I'd only seen in magazines—soft sable coats that smelled faintly of cedar, diamond chokers that sat cool and heavy against my throat, emerald drops that swung against my neckline when I moved. Every piece he fastened on me felt like a claim. I left them all behind in the walk-in closet he'd cleared for me on the second floor; I couldn't possibly explain them to my parents. "Late nights at the office," "a client dinner," "a colleague giving me a ride"—those excuses still worked. But the truth? That I was already picturing a life where I never went back to senior year, never sat through another lecture hall, never pretended I wanted anything except to belong to Victor Kane? That truth stayed locked behind my teeth.

I told myself it made perfect sense. School was supposed to lead to a job or a husband who could provide. Victor was both—wealthier than anyone I'd ever met, powerful in ways I only half-understood, and when he looked at me with those steel-gray eyes my whole body softened like butter left in the sun. He kept promising me a real place in "the organization." I believed him. I wanted to believe him.

* * *

I was proofreading a stack of correspondence when the door to the outer office opened without a knock.

"Hi there, gorgeous. Long time no see."

My head snapped up. My heart did a clumsy somersault.

He was leaning one hip against the edge of my desk— tall, lean, dark hair falling into warm brown eyes that seemed to see straight through the careful mask I'd been wearing all summer. Leather jacket, black button-down open at the throat, the faint scent of cedar and gun oil clinging to him. Dante Russo.

I felt my cheeks burn from throat to hairline. "H–hello," I managed. "Mr. Kane is… in a meeting."

Dante's mouth curved, slow and knowing. "Tell him his favorite associate is here."

I swallowed. There was something about the way he looked at me—gentle but piercing, like he could peel back every lie I'd ever told myself. It made me nervous. It made me wet between my thighs. And that terrified me because I already belonged to Victor. The thought of him finding out I'd even *noticed* another man made my stomach twist.

The intercom crackled. "Mia, is Dante out there?"

"Yes, sir."

"Send him in."

Dante pushed off the desk before I could speak, giving me a quick wink that felt like a secret shared between us. "Consider me sent."

I watched the door close behind him, my pulse loud in my ears. Before I could drag my attention back to the screen, the inner door opened again and Raven stepped out—long legs, seamed black stockings whispering with every movement, crimson lips curved in amusement.

She paused, studying me like I was something delicious she hadn't decided whether to bite yet.

"Victor says take a break, sweetheart," she purred, leaning over my desk so the deep V of her silk blouse framed the creamy swell of her breasts. "He wants you upstairs. I need help with something… personal."

My mouth went dry. "I still have—"

The intercom buzzed again.

"Mia." Victor's voice, low and final. "Go with Raven. I'll join you shortly."

"Yes, sir."

I saved the document, smoothed my skirt over my hips, and followed her. Raven's perfume—spicy vanilla and smoke—wrapped around me like a hand on the back of my neck.

* * *

Upstairs in the master bathroom, marble veined with gold, Raven didn't hesitate. She peeled off her bodycon dress, unhooked the black lace balconette bra, rolled the seamed stockings down her long legs with deliberate slowness, watching me watch her. Naked, she was breathtaking—full heavy breasts, cinched waist, the tiny raven tattoo on her hip like a signature. She turned on the taps; steaming water rushed into the oversized sunken tub, foam rising in thick clouds.

"My neck's been killing me," she said, scratching idly under one breast where the underwire had pressed. "Pinched nerve, maybe. I need heat… and hands." Her hazel eyes flicked to me. "Yours."

I couldn't look away. She was the only woman I'd ever seen like this—unashamed, powerful in her nakedness. The memory of her mouth on me weeks ago still lived under my skin, a low constant hum of want.

"Join me," she said, stepping into the water. Bubbles clung to her curves. "You won't get your pretty little outfit wet that way."

I stood frozen.

"Victor won't mind," she added softly. "He told you to help me, didn't he?"

That was the permission my body had been waiting for. My fingers shook as I unbuttoned my blouse, slid the skirt down my thighs, peeled off the pale lace panties Victor had chosen for me that morning. When I was bare, Raven's gaze moved over me like a physical touch—lingering on my small, high breasts, the soft blonde triangle between my legs, the faint freckles the sun had kissed across my shoulders.

"God, you're even lovelier than I remembered," she breathed.

My voice came out small. "So are you."

I stepped into the heat. The water enveloped me like a lover's arms; I sighed as it rose to my waist, then my breasts. Raven reached for the soap, lathered her palms, and began gliding them over my shoulders, my collarbones, cupping my breasts and rolling my nipples between slippery fingers until they ached and stood stiff.

"I thought *you* were the one who needed a massage," I whispered, half laughing, half trembling.

"I am," she murmured, thumbs circling my nipples. "But first I need to feel how soft you are. You make me ache, little one. You know that, don't you?"

Heat bloomed low in my belly. "Yes… and you…"

"What does she know?" Victor's deep voice rolled through the room like distant thunder.

We both turned. He stood in the doorway to the bedroom, shrugging off his suit jacket, loosening his tie with slow, deliberate movements. His eyes were dark with hunger.

"Meeting wrapped early," he said, unbuttoning his shirt to reveal the hard planes of his chest, silver threads gleaming among the dark hair. "Do you two want to be alone… or do you want company?"

Raven pouted playfully. "We hadn't even gotten to the massage part yet."

Victor's gaze dropped to the thick ridge already straining his trousers. "I've got something here that'll massage you both just fine."

I felt myself smile—slow, reckless. "Come in, Victor. The water's perfect."

Raven laughed low in her throat. "Join us, lover."

He shook his head. "Not enough room in there for what I have in mind. One of you might drown."

I giggled, stood—bubbles sliding down my body in slow, pearlescent trails—and stepped out of the tub. Water dripped from my nipples, my navel, the curls between my thighs. I walked straight to him, rose on tiptoe, and pressed my wet breasts to the crisp cotton still clinging to his chest.

"I hope you don't mind that we're soaked," I whispered.

Raven rose behind me, taller in her bare feet than I expected. She pressed close until her heavy breasts rested on my shoulders, framing my face in warm, soft flesh.

"Think you can handle both of us?" she taunted.

Victor's grin was feral. "If I can't, I'll die happy trying."

He took my hand and led me into the bedroom, Raven trailing behind like a shadow scented with sex. The king-sized bed was already turned down, sheets the color of midnight.

"The bed will get wet," I protested softly.

"Who gives a fuck?" Victor growled, dropping onto his back.

Raven pushed me aside with a playful shove. "Let's get these fucking pants off him."

Victor lifted his hips, smirking as we stripped him bare. His cock lay heavy against his thigh—thick, veined, already darkening with blood. My mouth watered.

"Who wants it first?" he asked.

"We both do," I breathed, crawling onto the bed and wrapping my fingers around him. He throbbed in my palm, hot and alive.

Raven stretched out on his other side, her crimson nails tracing his ribs. "When are you going to let her come work for me, Victor?"

"Shut it," he snapped. "Not now."

I froze. "What does she mean?"

"Nothing, baby." His arm curled around me, hand cupping my breast and squeezing until I gasped. "There are lots of ways a girl with your… talents can move up in the organization. We've talked about that."

"But I don't want to work for anyone else," I said, voice small.

"Easy." He pulled me closer, thumb brushing my nipple. "Raven just likes you. You'd still be mine. Understand?"

Raven leaned in, lips brushing my ear. "That's all, sweetheart. We could have so much fun together."

Victor changed the subject with a rough laugh. "Let's

have fun *now*. I've been thinking about the two of you naked and greedy for weeks."

Raven's hand covered mine on his cock. "Were they wet dreams?"

"Your pussies were dripping in them," he shot back.

She smiled at me. "You don't mind sharing, do you, pretty girl?"

I shook my head, dizzy with sudden heat. "No… not at all."

I leaned down and caught one of his flat nipples between my teeth, tugging gently. Raven mirrored me on the other side, tongue pushing deep into his ear.

"Fuck," Victor groaned, hands fisting in our hair. "You two are going to kill me."

He pushed our heads lower. "Mouths. Now. On my cock."

I kissed and nipped my way down his stomach, straddling his thigh so I could grind my slick folds against the hard muscle. My mouth hovered over his groin, circling closer, teasing. Raven did the same on his other side, dragging her cunt along his shin.

"My cock," he snarled. "Don't fucking tease."

We attacked together—tongues sliding up each side of the thick shaft, lips meeting at the swollen head, kissing around it, around each other. Spit slicked him, dripped down his balls. His hips jerked.

"Look at you two," he rasped. "Fucking gorgeous."

Raven purred against my mouth. "Isn't this fun, baby?"

"It's… incredible," I whimpered, giggling through the haze.

"Think this one cock's enough for both of us?" she teased.

I looked up at Victor, lips brushing his cockhead. "Maybe… maybe I'd like to taste Dante's too… if you didn't mind."

Victor barked a laugh. "I don't give a damn who you fuck as long as somebody drains my balls right now."

We laughed together, then went back to tormenting him—nipping, licking, slapping his shaft with wet tongues, french-kissing with his cock trapped between our mouths.

"You're fucking perfect," he groaned. "But I need a mouth. Now."

"Me!" I squealed. "Let me practice!"

Raven rolled him onto his side. "I'll tongue his ass while you suck his soul out."

She spread his cheeks and buried her face between them, tongue tracing the dark pucker before stabbing inside. Victor bucked, slamming his cock toward my mouth.

I opened wide. The fat head pushed past my lips, over my tongue, straight into my throat. I gagged, eyes watering, but the stretch, the roughness, the way he used me—it lit me up inside. My pussy clenched, dripping onto his thigh.

"Take it all, you little cocksucker," he growled, gripping my hair and fucking my face in short, brutal strokes.

I moaned around him, teeth grazing the base, fingers rolling his heavy balls. Raven's tongue plunged deeper into his ass; she scratched his thighs, chewed the tight ring.

Victor roared. "Fuck—yes—both of you—fuck!"

He hammered my throat. I choked, drooled, sucked harder. My cunt fluttered with every thrust, tiny orgasms flickering through me just from being used.

"I'm close—gonna fill your mouth, baby—"

We doubled down—my lips sealed tight, tongue whipping the underside, Raven's tongue fucking his ass, nails raking red lines across his skin.

"I'm coming!" he bellowed. "Drink it—fucking drink it!"

Hot, thick jets exploded across my tongue, down my throat. I gulped frantically, swallowing as much as I could while he held my head still and pumped. Come overflowed my lips, ran down my chin, dripped onto my breasts.

He finally rolled away, panting. "Jesus…"

Raven lunged, sealing her mouth to mine, sucking Victor's come from my tongue, my lips, my chin. She swallowed with a happy moan.

"You two," Victor rasped, watching us, "you are fucking unreal."

CHAPTER SEVEN

The air in Victor's private study still smelled of expensive cologne, cigar smoke, and the thick, musky perfume of arousal. My whole body felt liquid, humming, every nerve ending still sparkling from the way Dante had taken me earlier. But the hunger hadn't left me—it had only grown sharper, more desperate.

"It's our turn now," I heard myself say, voice high and breathy, almost a whine. I couldn't believe how shameless I sounded, but I didn't care. "You should take care of us, Victor."

Raven gave that slow, smoky laugh of hers, the one that always made heat pool low in my belly. "The girl's right," she purred, trailing one scarlet fingernail down the front of Victor's open shirt. "We're both aching to come again."

I reached for him first. His cock lay heavy and soft against his thigh, still glistening from Dante's mouth and my own earlier worship. I wrapped my small hand around it, feeling the warmth, the velvety weight. "Come on," I whispered, stroking gently, coaxing. "Get hard for us again."

Victor gave a low chuckle and caught Raven by the nape, guiding her glossy black head down. "Keep it in your mouth, darling," he told her, voice rough with command.

I watched, fascinated, as Raven's crimson lips parted and slid over him. The wet, obscene sucking sounds filled the room—slow, deliberate, luxurious. My clit throbbed in time with every slurp.

"Hurry, Raven," I moaned, unable to stay still. "Get him hard so he can fuck us."

I couldn't wait. I dropped down beside her, pressing my cheek to the hot, muscled plane of his thigh. My tongue darted out, lapping at the heavy sac beneath his cock, feeling the skin tighten, the balls drawing up under the wet velvet glide of my tongue. I massaged them softly, lovingly, tasting salt and man and the faint trace of what he'd already spilled earlier.

Victor's voice came out thick. "Who wants her ass fucked tonight?"

Raven's mouth came off him with a wet pop. "Me," she said instantly, voice husky. "I need it deep. I want that hot come enema filling me up."

Victor's gray eyes glittered. "Perfect. You can eat Mia's sweet little pussy while I ream your ass."

A shiver raced through me. I dragged my tongue in one long, slow stroke from the root of his cock all the way to the flushed head. He was already thickening, hardening, veins rising under my tongue like cords. I opened wide and took him deep, feeling the velvety steel fill my mouth, slide over my tongue, nudge the back of my throat. My eyes watered but I didn't care—I wanted him alive and pulsing again.

"Come on, Mia, hurry," Raven moaned, already

rocking back on her haunches. Victor's big hand was between her thighs, fingers sinking into her soaked cunt.

"Oooooh, yes, Victor," she gasped. "All of it—fist me, darling, open me wide."

I watched, dizzy, as he worked his whole hand into her. Five long fingers, then the knuckles, then the wrist—disappearing inside her stretched, glistening lips. He made a fist and began to pump, slow and deep. Raven's head fell back, mouth open in a silent scream of pleasure.

"He's hard now, baby," Victor told me, voice gravel. "Take that pretty mouth off."

I whimpered in protest but obeyed, letting his glistening cock spring free. "Let me put it in her," I begged, still clutching the thick shaft. "I want to watch it go in."

Raven was already moving—fluid, predatory—crawling onto hands and knees across the wide leather ottoman. Her heavy breasts swayed, nipples dark and stiff. Her ass lifted, cheeks parting slightly to show the shadowed pucker between. It twitched, hungry.

Victor knelt behind her. I held his cock steady, heart hammering so hard I could feel it in my throat. I dragged the swollen head through Raven's slick folds first, coating him in her juices, then guided him higher—right to that tight, pink ring.

"You ready?" Victor growled.

"Always, for you," Raven answered, pushing back.

"Fuck her, Victor," I moaned, rubbing my own dripping slit. "Fuck her ass deep."

He lunged. Raven hissed through her teeth as the fat head breached her, stretching the muscle wide. I watched, mesmerized, as inch after thick inch disappeared inside her.

"All of it," I breathed, fingers circling my clit. "Ram it all the way in."

Victor growled and drove forward, burying himself to the balls. Raven cried out, hips jerking.

"Yes!" I gasped, feeling faint. "Fuck her deep, Victor!"

He began to move—slow at first, savoring the vise-like grip of her ass. I scooted underneath Raven on my back, legs splayed wide, offering myself. My pussy was swollen, slick, aching.

Raven's hazel eyes locked on my glistening sex. "God, you're dripping," she murmured.

Victor's voice was dark velvet. "Go on, Raven. Eat her. I'll take care of your greedy little asshole."

He slammed in hard. Raven's whole body jolted, breasts swinging wildly. Then her mouth was on me— hot, wet, ravenous. Her tongue swept up my slit, curled around my clit, sucked hard. I screamed, hips bucking up into her face.

"Oooohhh, Raven!" I wailed. "Eat me—chew me— please!"

Victor pounded into her, hands gripping her hips, balls slapping wetly against her. "Bite her pretty pussy," he snarled.

Raven obeyed. Teeth grazed my clit, then closed—not breaking skin, just enough sharp pressure to make stars explode behind my eyes. I thrashed, grinding myself against her mouth.

"Yesssss!" I screamed. "Fuck her ass, Victor! Make her eat me harder!"

Raven moaned into my cunt, the vibration sending fresh waves through me. Her tongue stabbed deep, fucking me while Victor reamed her from behind. I could feel every brutal thrust travel through her body into mine.

"Make her come," Victor ordered, voice raw. "Make my little whore come."

The word *whore* hit me like a slap and a caress at once. My whole body clenched.

"Yes—make me come!" I begged. "Come all over your face, Raven!"

She sucked my clit hard, whipping the tip with her tongue. Her own hips jerked wildly, riding Victor's punishing cock. I felt her shudder, felt her cunt dripping onto the leather beneath us.

"I'm almost there!" I shrieked, clawing at the cushions. "Almost—"

"Bite her," Victor roared.

Raven's teeth sank in again and I shattered.

"I'm coming!" I screamed, voice breaking. "I'm commmmiiinnnggg!"

Hot, sweet juice gushed from me, flooding Raven's mouth. She drank greedily, moaning, while Victor hammered her ass faster, chasing his own release.

"I'm still coming!" I sobbed, back arched, nipples aching. "Make her come too, Victor—please!"

He snarled, pace brutal. Raven was trapped between us—my spasming cunt on her tongue, his thick cock splitting her ass. She began to shake violently.

"I'm there!" she gasped against my pussy. "I'm coming—fuck—coming so hard!"

Victor roared. "Take it!"

I watched his balls tighten, saw the moment he erupted. Thick ropes of come blasted deep into Raven's bowels. She screamed into my cunt, body convulsing, milking him with her ass while her own orgasm tore through her.

Jizz and her juices ran down her thighs. I reached up, pinched her swollen clit, rubbed Victor's churning balls with my come-slick fingers.

"Cream her ass," I chanted. "Fill her up!"

Victor gave one last savage thrust, emptying everything into her. Raven collapsed forward, face pressed to my thigh, whimpering as the last spasms rolled through her.

Victor pulled out slowly. Creamy white seeped from her gaping hole.

He looked down at me, eyes dark. "Clean her up, Mia. You'll love the taste."

I didn't hesitate. I crawled behind Raven, spread her cheeks, and fastened my mouth to her ruined asshole. Hot, salty come poured onto my tongue. I sucked hungrily, swallowing, then pushed my tongue inside, scooping out every drop.

Raven sighed weakly. "Yes, baby… clean me… so good…"

When I'd licked her clean, I sat back, lips swollen, face flushed, pussy still twitching.

I looked at Victor's cock—softening but still massive—and reached for it. "Can you get hard again?" I whispered. "I need you inside me so badly."

He gave that slow, dangerous smile. "I'll get hard, kitten. But maybe we should call Dante back in. Wouldn't want to wear your old man out completely."

Raven laughed softly, rolling onto her side. "Yes… let's bring the pretty cop in. I want to see him fuck our little blonde angel again."

I stroked Victor's cock, feeling it twitch under my fingers. "I love you," I breathed, dizzy with sex and stupid, dangerous happiness.

Victor grunted, brushing a thumb across my swollen lower lip. "Sure you do, baby. Sure you do."

CHAPTER EIGHT

Fucking Victor had become the center of my world, the only thing that felt real anymore. Every time he took me—hard, slow, rough, tender—I discovered new layers of myself I never knew existed. My body learned to crave the stretch, the burn, the way my pussy clenched and fluttered when he filled me completely. But I also learned things about my soul that made my cheeks burn with shame even as my cunt dripped with fresh heat. I wasn't the good girl I'd always pretended to be. Honor? Loyalty? Those words felt distant, silly, when his thick cock was buried inside me and my mind went blank with bliss.

When Victor first mentioned I might "entertain" some of his out-of-town associates—men with heavy watches and colder eyes—I barely hesitated. A tiny flicker of unease, quickly drowned by the memory of his hands on my throat, his teeth on my nipple, the way he growled "good girl" when I came so hard I saw stars. I told myself it was just business. I told myself I loved him. I told myself anything to keep the sick-sweet ache between my legs from stopping.

Whenever doubt crept in—when I overheard him on the phone, voice low and lethal, promising to "handle" someone who crossed him—I turned away. I pressed my thighs together, felt the damp silk of my panties cling, and hurried to find him. I'd tear at his belt, drop to my knees, or climb onto his lap right there in his study, riding him until the questions burned away in the white-hot rush of orgasm. The more we fucked, the more desperately I needed him. Yet the more I gave, the colder he became. Lately when he fucked me it felt mechanical, like I was just a warm, wet sleeve for his cock. No kisses. No whispered filth. Just deep, relentless thrusts that left me shaking and empty the moment he pulled out.

One humid morning Victor was gone—some meeting with men I'd never met. The estate felt too quiet, too vast. I swam alone in the infinity pool, the water cool against my overheated skin, then padded upstairs to the guest suite I'd claimed as my own. The walk-in closet was a treasure cave of everything he'd bought me: silk slips, garter belts, sky-high Louboutins, dresses so sheer they hid nothing. I loved trying them on, twirling in front of the full-length mirror, watching my breasts jiggle, my nipples pebble under lace, my ass flex in tiny thongs. Today I chose sporty-luxe: tiny white shorts that rode high and dug cruelly into my swollen pussy lips, the seam pressing right against my clit with every step. I paired them with a barely-there halter top—two triangles of soft cotton that covered my nipples and little else. My long blonde hair spilled loose down my back, still damp from the pool. I ran my palms over my body—down my ribs, over the sensitive undersides of my breasts, across the flat plane of my stomach, then cupped my mound through the thin fabric. A shiver raced through me. I looked like sin dressed up as summer.

Bored and restless, my skin tingling with unmet need, I wandered the house. Downstairs I heard a faint rustle from the direction of my little office—the one attached to Victor's private sanctum. My pulse kicked up. No one was supposed to be here. Burglar? Intruder? The thought sent a dark thrill straight to my core. What would it feel like, I wondered, to be shoved against the desk, skirt hiked, panties ripped aside, taken hard and fast by someone who didn't ask permission? My pussy clenched at the fantasy, a fresh gush of wetness soaking the crotch of my shorts.

I crept to the door on bare feet, heart hammering. The inner door to Victor's office stood slightly ajar. Through the crack I saw him—Dante Russo—methodically rifling through drawers.

"Dante?" My voice came out higher than I intended.

His hand flashed; in an instant a sleek black pistol was trained on my chest.

I threw my hands up. "Wait! It's just me!"

Recognition flickered. He lowered the gun slowly, sliding it back into his shoulder holster. "Mia. Jesus. You scared the hell out of me."

"What are you doing here?" I asked, still trembling. "Why are you in Victor's desk?"

He closed the last drawer, stepped around the desk. "Looking for some documents I left last week. Needed them for a deal." He guided me gently backward into the reception area and shut the connecting door. "Didn't realize anyone was home."

"I didn't hear you come in," I said, confused, my nipples stiff against the thin halter from the adrenaline and the cool air.

"Let myself in with the code. Thought the place was empty." His gaze dropped, sweeping over me—lingering on the way the shorts cut into my hips, the sliver of underboob exposed by the halter. "You're looking… incredible today."

I gave a little model's spin, feeling the fabric ride higher, the seam rubbing my clit. "Just playing dress-up. New outfit. Do you like?" I bit my lip, struck a coy pose with one finger between my teeth.

"Very dangerous outfit for wandering around alone," he said, voice roughening. "Especially if a stranger decided to take advantage."

The words landed low in my belly. I stepped closer, pushed him down into one of the deep leather chairs, then straddled his lap without asking. "I've been thinking about you," I whispered. "Why haven't you come to see me?"

His hands settled on my hips, fingers digging in just enough to make me gasp. I could feel him hardening beneath me, thick and insistent. "Thought you belonged to Victor."

I giggled, rocking my soaked pussy against the growing ridge in his jeans. "Victor doesn't own me." I leaned in, brushing my lips over his. "I told him you're cute. He didn't mind."

Dante exhaled sharply. I covered his mouth with

mine, tongue slipping in, hungry and bold. He froze for a heartbeat—then his arms banded around me, pulling me tighter as he kissed back, deep and devouring.

"You'd better be careful, little girl," he growled against my lips, "or you'll get exactly what you're asking for."

I flicked my tongue across his lower lip, grinding harder. "Maybe I want it rough."

His eyes darkened. "What has Victor been teaching you?"

"Everything," I breathed, running my tongue up the side of his neck. "How to take it. How to beg for it. How to love it when it hurts."

He groaned. I felt his control fraying.

"Call me names," I whispered. "Tell me what I am."

"You're playing with fire, Mia."

I reached between us, palmed the thick length straining his jeans. "You've got a hard cock. Do you want to fuck me?"

Something snapped. He flipped me over his knee in one smooth motion, ass up, shorts stretched tight. His palm cracked down—hard.

I yelped, then moaned. "Yes! Again!"

"Slut," he snarled, spanking harder. "Little whore."

Each slap sent fire through my cheeks, straight to my dripping cunt. "Yes! I'm your whore! Beat me!"

He tore the shorts down my thighs, leaving them tangled at my knees. Another barrage—bare skin now, stinging, blooming pink. I writhed, spreading my legs, offering everything.

"Feel how wet I am," I begged. "Please—touch me!"

His fingers found my swollen lips, slipped through slick heat. I spasmed, creaming instantly.

I rolled off his lap, stood on shaky legs, peeled the halter over my head. Naked except for the twisted shorts around my knees, I turned slowly, showing him the glowing red handprints on my ass.

"It hurts so good," I purred. "Call me your dirty little slut again."

He lunged, tackling me to the thick carpet. His mouth crashed onto mine, savage. I clawed at his shirt, humping up against him as he bit down my neck, my shoulders, then latched onto my breast—sucking hard, then teeth closing on the tender nipple.

I arched, wailing. "Bite me! Harder!"

He mauled my tits, switching sides, leaving marks. Pain and pleasure twisted together until I was shaking, pussy gushing.

He slid down, shoved my thighs wide, buried his face in me. Tongue plunging deep, lips sucking my folds, teeth grazing my clit. I screamed, bucking.

"Finger my ass!" I begged. "Hurt me! Make me come!"

One thick finger breached my tight ring. He sucked my clit brutally, twisting, biting just enough to send me over. I shattered—screaming his name, flooding his mouth, ass clenching around his invading finger as wave after wave ripped through me.

He kept going—relentless—until I collapsed, twitching, drooling, limp in ecstasy.

I smiled up at him through dazed eyes, licking my swollen lips. "Now let me take care of you, Dante. I'll take such good care of you…"

CHAPTER NINE

I sat up slowly, every nerve in my body humming like a live wire. The silk of my stockings whispered against the leather couch as I shifted, the sheer black fabric clinging to my thighs, still damp from earlier exertions. My heart pounded so hard I could feel it in my throat, in my fingertips, in the swollen, aching place between my legs. Dante lay there watching me, his dark eyes heavy-lidded, that lazy half-smile playing on his lips—the kind that made my stomach flip even now.

"Let me get your clothes off," I whispered, licking my suddenly dry lips. My voice came out breathy, needy, nothing like the careful, polite girl who'd answered Victor's ad for a summer secretary.

Dante's smile widened. He didn't move to help; he just watched as my trembling fingers attacked the buttons of his dark shirt, then tugged at his belt, frantic, clumsy with want. Fabric tore a little—I didn't care. In seconds he was bare, sprawled back against the cushions of Victor's private study, his thick cock standing rigid from his groin, veined and flushed, pulsing with every beat of his heart. The sight stole my breath. Heat flooded my cheeks, my chest, pooled low in my belly until I felt slick and empty all at once.

"It's all yours, kitten," he murmured, folding his hands behind his head, the muscles in his arms and chest flexing under olive skin. His voice was rough, amused, but the way his cock twitched told me everything I needed to know.

I nearly whimpered aloud. Just looking at it—thick, heavy, glistening at the tip—rekindled the fire that had barely cooled from when he'd had me on my knees earlier. My nipples tightened painfully against the thin lace of my bra, and fresh wetness seeped between my thighs, soaking the crotch of my panties beneath the garter belt. "Just looking at your cock makes me so hungry," I breathed, the words spilling out before I could stop them. They sounded filthy coming from my mouth, but they felt true. "And I've got a treat for you."

"What's that, baby?" He stayed relaxed, but his eyes darkened, tracking the sway of my breasts as I leaned closer.

I gave him a small, wicked smile—the kind Raven had taught me in front of the mirror last week. "I'm going to let you fuck my virgin ass."

His breath caught. "Thought nothing on you was virgin anymore."

"Oh yes," I giggled, low and dirty, surprising even myself. "I saved my asshole for someone special. Someone like you."

I swooped down before he could answer, pressing hot, open-mouthed kisses along his tight lower belly, inhaling the musky male scent of him mixed with the faint leather of his jacket. My tongue traced the line of hair leading down from his navel. Every lick sent shivers racing up my own spine; my clit throbbed in time with my heartbeat.

"Go for it, kitten," he rasped, voice thicker now.

I slithered over him like liquid heat, my stockinged legs straddling one of his thighs so I could grind my soaked pussy against the hard muscle there while I worked. I licked and nibbled his chest, caught one flat nipple between my teeth and tugged until he hissed. My hands roamed everywhere—scratching lightly down his sides, kneading the taut flesh of his abdomen, feeling him tense and shudder under my touch. My breasts dragged over his skin, nipples scraping deliciously, sending sparks straight to my core.

"You're a wild little thing," he groaned, hips lifting slightly. "A real sex kitten in silk."

The praise made me moan. I slid lower, trapping his burning cock between my breasts, squeezing them together so the hot length slid through the soft valley. The friction was exquisite—velvet skin over steel—and I could feel every vein pulsing against me. "Your cock's so hot," I whimpered, rocking gently. "It's burning right through my tits."

"It'll burn your ass too," he promised, voice dark with hunger. "But first—use that pretty mouth. Suck me, Mia."

The command sent a fresh gush of wetness down my thighs. "Soon," I teased, smiling up at him through my lashes. "I can hardly wait to taste all your come flooding my mouth again."

I twisted around and settled between his spread legs, the silk of my stockings rasping against the rug. A needy sound escaped me as I kissed the sensitive skin of his inner thigh, then higher, licking and nipping until I reached the heavy sac of his balls. I soaked them with slow, wet strokes of my tongue, feeling them tighten and draw up under my attention. Then lower still, nibbling the tender crease where thigh met ass, shameless, lost in the taste and scent of him.

"Goddamn, you're incredible," he groaned, hips jerking. "Where'd a sweet girl like you learn to please a man like this?"

"It comes naturally," I purred against his skin. "I'm just a natural-born cocksucker."

The word felt wicked and right on my tongue. He snarled softly. "Then get to work and suck, you little bitch."

The filthy name hit me like a caress. I worked my mouth up the thick shaft, biting gently, gnawing my way slowly toward the swollen head. I kissed and licked every inch, trailing saliva that gleamed in the low lamplight. When I reached the tip I swirled my tongue around it in a lewd, open-mouthed kiss.

"Stop teasing," he gasped, voice strained. "Or I'll spank that perfect ass red again."

"You already did," I reminded him breathlessly, "and I loved every stinging slap, remember?"

I dove back down, licking and sucking along the

pulsing length until he was groaning, hips bucking. "In your mouth, kitten. Now."

I giggled—high, lewd, dizzy with power—and dodged his upward thrusts for a moment longer, making him chase my lips. "Stop moving and I'll suck you properly," I taunted. "

His eyes flashed. "Suck it, whore. Suck my cock, you filthy little cocksucking bitch."

The words ignited me. I opened wide and took the spongy head inside, sealing my lips tight and swirling my tongue around the ridge. The salty taste of pre-come bloomed on my tongue; I moaned around him, cheeks hollowing as I sucked hard.

"Oh fuck, Mia—" His hips jerked, driving deeper.

I let him push, relaxing my throat until my nose pressed into the coarse hair at his base. I gagged, eyes watering, but the stretch, the fullness, the way my throat fluttered around him—it was perfect. Spit dripped from my lips, ran down his shaft, pooled at his balls. I eased back slowly, scraping my teeth lightly along the underside, then slammed down again, fucking my face on his cock with desperate rhythm.

He caught the pace, thrusting up to meet me, groaning my name like a prayer. His cock swelled impossibly thicker, hotter. I grabbed his balls, rolling and tugging them, feeling them churn under my palms.

"I'm close, baby," he growled. "Use that tongue—suck me off. I wanna come down your greedy throat."

I shuddered, my own pussy clenching on nothing,

dripping steadily onto the rug. I drove down hard, held him deep, squeezed his balls rhythmically—and he broke.

"Here it comes—fuck—drink it, you bitch!"

Hot, thick spurts flooded my throat. I swallowed convulsively, gulping the salty flood, milking him with throat and hands. Come overflowed, dribbling from the corners of my mouth, running down my chin, splattering my heaving breasts. Another pulse, another—his hips slammed up, battering my face with his groin as he roared through it.

I kept sucking, frantic, greedy, until he collapsed back, gasping. One last thick rope slid onto my tongue; I savored it, then popped off with a wet sound, licking my swollen lips.

He stared at me, dazed, chest heaving. "Where the hell did you learn to suck cock like that?"

I smiled, bright and filthy, wiping a stray drop from my chin with one finger and sucking it clean. "I've been practicing all summer. Victor says I could make a real career of it."

He laughed, low and rough, still catching his breath. "Anyone can make a career of fucking, kitten. You've got other qualities too."

I crawled up his body, straddling his hips, letting my dripping pussy slide along his softening cock. "I've got at least one quality I want you to fuck right now." My voice dropped to a needy whisper. "My ass is still virgin… and it's aching for you."

CHAPTER TEN

My pussy was on fire, a hot, throbbing ache that pulsed deep between my thighs as I squirmed in Dante Russo's strong arms, my lithe young body still slick with sweat and my own creamy juices. The thick Persian carpet in Victor Kane's private study felt plush against my skin, but nothing could cool the molten need inside me. "My pussy's so hot, Dante," I purred, my voice breathy and trembling, pressing my small breasts against his muscular chest. "Are you like this all the time?" he asked, his warm brown eyes dark with lust. "Or am I just lucky?"

"Both," I sighed, snuggling closer, my long blonde hair spilling like silk over his shoulder. "I'm like this so much lately… and I think I like you, Dante. Really like you."

He stroked my back, but I saw the flicker of concern in his gaze. "That's sweet, Mia. But I thought you were Victor's girl."

I blushed, averting my eyes, my cheeks burning. "We started that way… but he keeps talking about me dating his business associates. For money, maybe? I don't know." My voice dropped to a whisper. "He says they'd pay a lot for a girl like me."

"Don't do it, Mia," Dante said firmly, his arms tightening around me. "You're too sweet for that world. You wouldn't like it."

I didn't want to think about Victor or his threats right

now. My body was screaming for more. "I like you," I murmured, changing the subject with a wicked little smile. "I love the way you made me come."

I slithered out of his embrace and straddled his powerful frame, grinding my dripping pussy against his chest, leaving a wet trail of my excitement on his skin. The heat of him made my clit throb. "I want you to have my asshole now," I said brightly, my blue eyes sparkling with naughty innocence. "I've been saving it… and I decided I want you to be the first."

Before he could answer, I covered his mouth with mine, shoving my tongue deep, tasting him as I rubbed my slick folds along his thigh. My mind spun with filthy images—his thick cock stretching my virgin ass until I screamed. He groaned into my kiss, fingers tangling in my hair, mashing my face down toward his groin. I knew he was fighting his better judgment, but his cock was already twitching, swelling for me. I felt powerful, wanted, utterly alive.

My lips found his semi-hard shaft and I kissed it hungrily, then chewed gently along the thickening length. My hips rolled, dragging my soaked cunt back and forth over his knee, the friction making sparks explode behind my eyes. "Suck it good, baby," he rasped, holding my head in place.

I did. I gobbled him down until my nose pressed into his dark curls, my throat bulging around his rigid cock. Spit drooled from the corners of my mouth as I sucked frantically, feeling him grow rock-hard against my tongue. When I finally popped off, gasping, I stared at the towering monster in awe. "God, it's so hard again…"

Trembling, I crawled onto my hands and knees on the thick carpet, presenting my firm little ass to him, my pert C-cup breasts dangling and swaying.

"Fuck me, Dante," I cooed, wiggling my heart-shaped bottom. "But first… play with my feet. I want to feel you between them."

His eyes darkened with surprise and raw hunger. He grabbed my ankles gently and lifted my stocking-clad feet toward his throbbing cock. The heat of his shaft pressed between the silky arches of my small soles, and oh God—the sensation was electric. The sheer silk stretched taut over my toes as he started to thrust, slow and deliberate, fucking my feet like they were a tight little pussy. Every slide sent shivers racing up my legs straight to my dripping cunt. The smooth, luxurious friction of the stockings against his veiny cock made my toes curl inside the silk, the delicate material bunching and gliding in the most delicious way.

"Mmm, Mia… these silk stockings feel like heaven," he groaned, his voice thick. He sucked my toes one by one, right through the sheer fabric, his hot tongue swirling around each sensitive digit. The wet heat soaked the silk, making it cling even tighter, and I whimpered helplessly. My pussy clenched and gushed fresh cream down my thighs. I never knew my feet could feel so dirty, so adored. The silky barrier made every lick and suck feel wickedly forbidden—my toes throbbed with pleasure, little sparks shooting straight to my clit until I was shaking. "I love it," I gasped, my voice breaking. "Suck my stocking toes harder, Dante… fuck my feet… it makes my pussy so wet!"

He pumped faster between my arches, the silk growing slick with his pre-come, the obscene wet sounds filling the study. My whole body flushed hot; the stockings turned my innocent little feet into something slutty and irresistible. I came just from that—tiny, fluttering spasms rippling through my cunt without him even touching it.

Then he flipped me onto my back for a moment, still sucking greedily at my silk-wrapped toes while he dragged his cockhead through my seeping pussy lips, greasing himself. "Your cunt's sweet, baby," he rasped. "But now… that ass."

I rolled over again, arching high on all fours, stockings still gleaming on my legs. He pushed forward, stretching my virgin asshole inch by burning inch. The pain was sharp at first, a white-hot tear that made me scream, but it melted into the deepest, fullest pleasure I'd ever felt. My silk-clad toes dug into the carpet as he buried himself to the balls, my ass clenching around him like a velvet fist. Every thrust made the stockings whisper against my skin, reminding me of the foot-fucking that had just set me on fire.

I fucked myself back on him wildly, stockings taut over my calves, toes curling in ecstasy. My pussy poured juice down my thighs, soaking the garter straps. "Harder, Dante! Fuck my ass! I'm coming again!" Wave after wave crashed through me, my body a quivering mess of silk and sweat and pure sensation. When he finally roared and flooded my bowels with thick, hot spurts of come, I felt every pulse deep inside, the silky heat of it making my toes curl so hard the stockings strained.

Afterward, he eased out, and I scrambled up. I licked and sucked his softening cock clean, tasting my ass and his jizz, purring like a contented kitten. "I love your cock, Dante," I whispered. "I love you."

"Well, well, well." Victor Kane's deep voice sliced through the air from the doorway like a knife.

I jerked upright, eyes wide, heart hammering. Dante tensed beside me.

"Just what the hell do you think you're doing here?" Victor snarled, stepping into his own study, his steel-gray eyes blazing.

"Victor! Don't be mad… it was my fault…" I stammered, trying to cover my naked breasts with trembling hands.

Dante stood, reaching for his clothes. "Hold it right there!" Victor barked. "What the fuck were you doing in my office, Russo?"

"Hey, boss," Dante tried, casual as he could. "I came to see you and Mia here… I couldn't keep my hands off her. Sorry."

"No, Victor," I interrupted, tears already stinging my eyes. "It was all my fault!"

"Shut up, bitch!" Victor roared, slapping me viciously across the mouth. I collapsed onto the carpet, tasting blood, sobbing quietly, the sheer silk of my stockings now damp with my tears and come.

Dante moved, but Victor's boot slammed into his groin. Dante crumpled, groaning. Victor pulled a gun, eyes wild as he ransacked his desk. "Where the fuck is my appointment book?" he bellowed. "You stole my whole delivery schedule, you little whore! Planning to sell it to the cops?"

He swung the gun toward me. Dante dove for his jacket, rolling across the floor. A shot cracked—plaster exploded from the wall. Dante fired back from behind the couch. The bullet slammed into Victor's ribs. He went down behind the desk, moaning.

"Throw the gun out, Kane!" Dante yelled. "I'm with the D.A.'s office—you're under arrest!"

Victor's gun skittered across the carpet. I crawled behind Dante, shaking, still in nothing but my garter-belt and silk stockings.

"Am I under arrest too?" I whispered, voice tiny.

"No, baby," Dante said softly, pulling me close, his arm warm around my trembling shoulders. "You didn't know what you were getting into. Don't worry… I'll take care of you."

I pressed my face into his chest, the silk of my stockings whispering against my skin as I clung to him. And I'll take care of you, Dante, I thought, a dark little smile touching my swollen lips. I'll take care of you until you scream for mercy.

THE END

A Story from

Yesteryear's Stories Reflected Today
Yabot AB
www.yabot.se/en